COLLECTION
— OF —
STORYTIME
FAVORITES

HarperCollins*Publishers*

COLLECTION
— OF —
STORYTIME
FAVORITES

HarperCollins*Publishers*

AND I
MEAN IT,
STANLEY

An I Can Read Book®

AND I MEAN IT, STANLEY

by CROSBY BONSALL

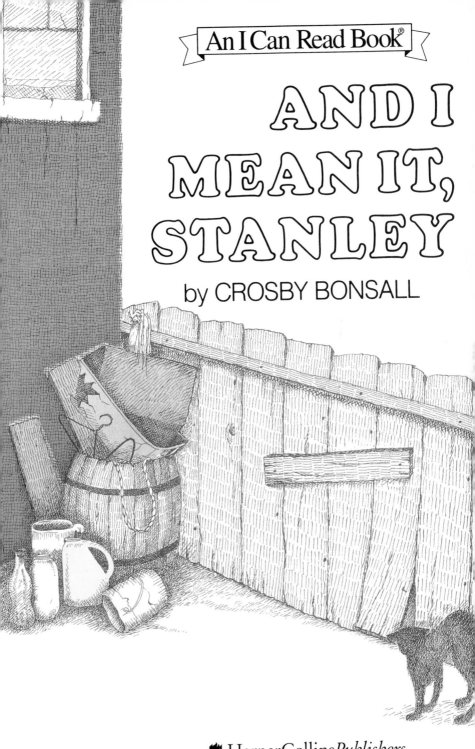

HarperCollins*Publishers*

Listen, Stanley.

I know you are there.

I know you are

in back of the fence.

But I don't care, Stanley.

I don't want to play with you.

I don't want to talk to you.

You stay there, Stanley.

Stay in back of the fence.

I don't care.

I can play by myself, Stanley.

I don't need you, Stanley.

And I mean it, Stanley.

I am having a lot of fun.

A lot of fun!

I am making a great thing, Stanley.

A really, truly great thing.

And when it is done,

you will want to see it, Stanley.

Well, you can't.

I don't want you to.

And I mean it, Stanley.

I don't want you to see
what I am making.

You stay there, Stanley.

Don't you look.

Don't you look.

Don't even peek.

You hear me, Stanley?

This thing I am making

is really neat.

It is really neat, Stanley.

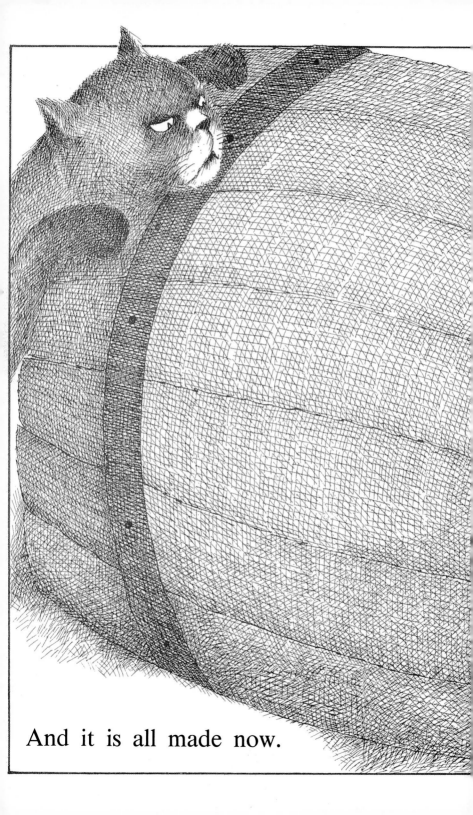

And it is all made now.

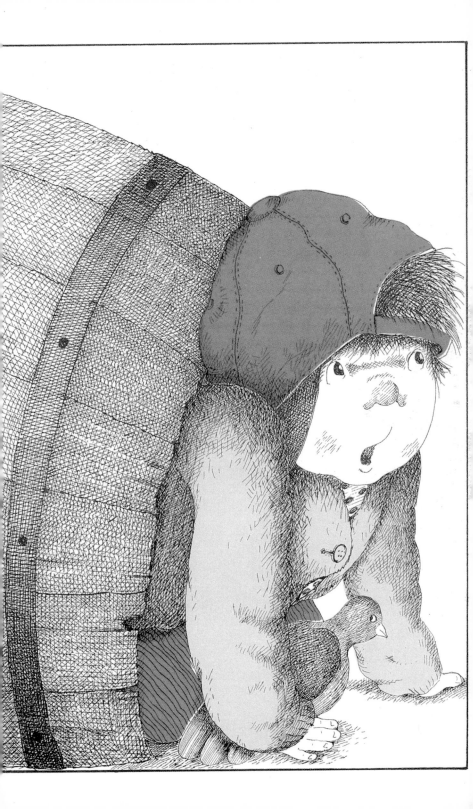

The very best thing I ever made.

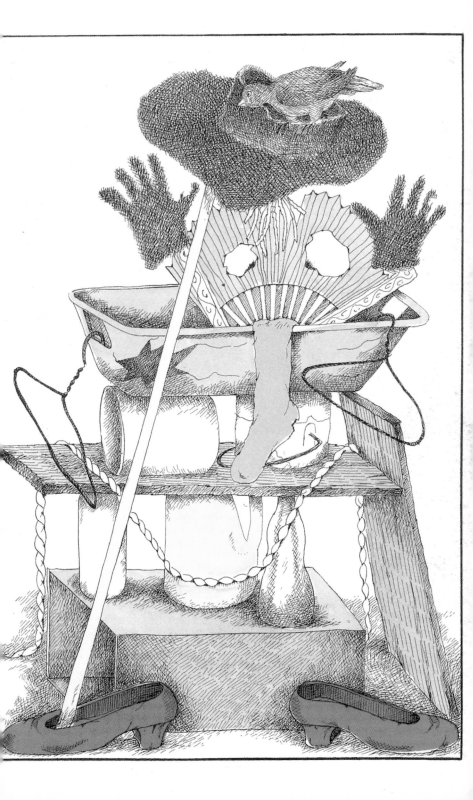

But don't you look, Stanley.

I don't want you to see it.

And I mean it. . .

STANLEY!

Aw, Stanley.

THE FAT CAT SAT ON THE MAT

written and illustrated by
NURIT KARLIN

HarperCollins*Publishers*

To Shira and Zohar

Wilma the witch has a crazy broom.

It likes to fly around her room.

She also has a fat cat

and a pet rat.

Wilma loves her pet rat.

She calls the rat

"my little brat."

The rat hates the cat.

The cat does not care.

The cat, who is fat,

just lies in the vat

and stares at the rat.

The rat hates that.

One night, when Wilma was out,

the fat cat got out of the vat.

He went, *pit-a-pat*,

and sat on the mat.

"This is MY mat!" said the rat.

"So what," said the cat.

"So get off!" said the rat.

"No I won't," said the cat.

"Then I will go and get my bat,"
said the rat.

"It will get you off the mat."

"No it won't," said the cat.

"This is the mat of the rat,"
said the bat.

"So what," said the cat.

"So get off!" said the bat.

"No I won't," said the cat.

"Then I will go and get my hat,"
said the bat.

"It will get you off the mat."

"No it won't," said the cat.

"This is the mat of the rat,"
said the hat.

"So what," said the cat.

"So get off!" said the hat.

"No I won't," said the cat.

"I am a cat, and I am fat.
No rat, no bat, no hat
can move me.
I shall sit on this mat
for as long as I wish."

"We shall see," said the hat.

"Look what we have," said the hat.

"Big deal, a dish," said the cat.

"A dish and what else?" asked the hat.

"Mmmm . . . a fish!" said the cat.

"A fish on a dish," said the hat.

"For me?" asked the cat.

"Yes, for you," said the hat.

"Bring it closer," said the cat.

"Come and get it," said the hat.

"You think I am stupid,"
said the cat.
"You want to get me off the mat.
I won't get off, and that is that!"

Rat-a-tat . . .

"What was that?" asked the bat.

"I don't know," said the hat.

Rat-a-tat . . .

"It sounds like a rat with a tat,"
said the cat.

"It is not me," said the rat.

"What is a tat?" asked the bat.

"I don't know," said the hat.

"Look! The broom!" cried the bat.

The broom flew into the room.

It zoomed over the mat,

over the cat,

over the hat and the bat

and Wilma's pet rat.

The fish flew off the dish.

23

It landed on the hat,

which landed on the bat,

who landed on the rat,

who landed on the cat,

lying flat on the mat.

"Get off!" said the cat.

"No we won't!" said the hat

and the bat and the rat.

The fish said nothing.

Wilma came home.

She looked at the room.

She picked up the broom.

Then she asked,

"Why is the fish out of the dish?"

"Because of the cat," said the rat.

"The fat cat sat on my mat!"

"My dear little brat," said Wilma,
"what makes you think
this is YOUR mat?"

The fat cat smiled.

The fat cat got up

and stretched.

Off flew the rat, the bat,

and the hat.

He ate the fish,

licked the dish,

and went back

to lie down in the vat.

"Thank goodness!"

said the mat.

HARRY
and the
Lady Next Door

HARRY and

Pictures by
Margaret Bloy Graham

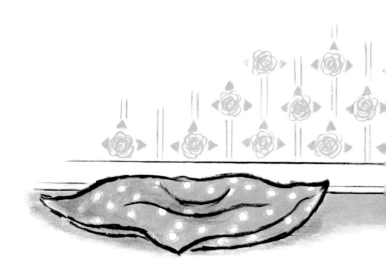

the Lady Next Door

by Gene Zion

HarperCollins*Publishers*

THE PARTY

Harry was a white dog

with black spots.

He loved all his neighbors,

all except one.

He did not love the lady next door.

The lady next door sang.

She sang high and loud.

When she sang, Harry's ears hurt.

She sang higher
than the peanut whistle.
When she sang, the peanut man
put his hands over his ears.

She sang louder

than the siren on the fire engine.

When she sang, the firemen

put their hands over their ears.

She sang higher and louder

than the cats sang.

When she sang, the cats ran away.

Harry tried everything to make her stop.

He howled under her window.

His friends howled too.

But it did not do any good.

The lady next door went on singing.

She sang higher and louder than ever.

One day Harry's family gave a party.

They invited the lady next door.

She came with her music.

When she started to sing,

Harry almost bit her leg.

But he bit the leg of the piano instead.

The family sent Harry

out of the room.

"You are a bad dog,"

they said.

Harry just wagged his tail.

As he walked to the door
some people said,
"Poor Harry."
But others whispered,
"The lucky dog!"

When Harry pushed the door open
the wind blew in.
It blew the pages of music off the piano.
They blew all around the room.
Everyone tried to catch the music
but no one could.

The pages blew out the door
and into the garden.
They blew over the fence
and up into the trees.
Harry caught some of the pages
but he did not bring them back.
He ran away with them.

HARRY'S FIRST TRY

He ran until he came to a quiet spot.

He dropped the music and lay down.

Soon he fell asleep.

In a little while,

something woke Harry up.

All around him were cows mooing.

They mooed very low notes.

Harry listened.

He thought the cows

made beautiful music.

He had never heard anything
so soft and low.
He wished the lady next door
would sing like the cows.
Suddenly Harry had an idea.

He rounded up all the cows.

He barked at their heels.

Down the road they went.

Harry barked and the cows mooed.

They ran on and on.

They ran down the main street of town.

They passed the school, the library

and the fire house.

When they came to Harry's house

the lady was still singing.

Harry ran ahead and stopped the cows.

They went on mooing.

They mooed and mooed and mooed.

They all mooed soft and low.

The cows mooed for a long time

but it did not do any good.

The lady next door went on singing.

She sang higher and louder than ever.

Harry's family called the man

who owned the cows.

He came and took them home.

That night,

Harry slept in the dog house.

HARRY'S SECOND TRY

The next day

the lady next door sang some more.

Harry's ears hurt more than ever.

He went for a walk.

After he had walked for a long time

he heard a wonderful sound.

"Oompah! Oompah! Oompah! Oompah!"

It was low and lovely.

Then Harry saw what it was.

It was the big horn

in the Firemen's Band.

The big horn was even softer and lower

than cows mooing.

Harry walked along listening.

He wished the lady next door

would sing like the big horn.

Then he saw the leader of the band.

The leader threw his stick into the air.

Harry watched.

Suddenly he had an idea.

The next time

the stick went into the air,

Harry caught it.

Harry ran in front of the band.

The leader ran after Harry—

and the band ran after the leader.

Soon the leader was all out of breath.

He stopped running.

But the band ran after Harry.

The men played as they ran.

Harry led them all

down the main street of town.

They passed the school, the library

and the fire house.

Harry stopped the band

in front of the lady's house.

She was still singing.

The big horn player played

even softer and lower than before.

He blew and blew and blew

right under her window.

But it did not do any good.

The lady next door went on singing.

She sang higher and louder than ever.

When the leader got there

he had Harry's family with him.

Harry gave the stick back.

That night,

he slept in the dog house again.

THE CONTEST

A few nights after that,

the family took Harry to the park.

They were going to hear

the Firemen's Band.

The family knew that Harry liked

the big horn.

They got to the park and sat down.

A light shone on the stage.

The people were quiet.

They waited for the music to begin.

Harry closed his eyes and listened.

He waited for the big horn.

He waited for the soft, low notes.

But the low notes never came.

Instead, a man came out.

"Good evening, friends," he said.

"The band will not play tonight.

The big horn player is all out of breath.

Instead, we shall have a singing contest.

And here are the ladies who will sing."

Everyone clapped
when the ladies came out.
On the end of the line
was the lady next door.
Harry took one look
and ran off.

45

He was almost out of the park

when he heard something.

"Blurp Blurp."

"Blurp Blurp."

It was low and beautiful.

Harry stopped and listened.

It was even softer and lower

than the cows and the big horn.

He wished the lady next door

would sing like this.

Then he saw where the sound came from.

It came from inside a watering can.

Suddenly Harry had an idea.

He took the handle of the can

in his mouth.

Then he ran with it.

When he got back to the bandstand,

he walked quietly up the stairs.

The lady next door was singing.

Harry put the watering can

on the floor behind her.

Soon the lady sang a *very* high note.

Then something happened.

Two frogs jumped out of the can.

One jumped on the lady's head.

The other jumped on her shoulder.

The other ladies in the contest

shrieked and ran from the stage.

But the lady next door went on singing.

She sang higher and louder than ever.

When she finished her song,

everyone shouted, "Hooray!"

The judges whispered together.

Then one of them spoke.

"Ladies and gentlemen," he said.

"The other ladies in the contest

have all gone home.

So the lady next door wins

the singing contest!

She is a *brave* lady.

She wins First Prize.

It means she can study music

in a far-off country

for a long time!"

Everyone clapped and clapped.

Harry barked and barked.

He was the happiest of all.

In the middle of all the fuss

the frogs hopped home.

Soon the time came

for the lady next door

to go away.

Harry went to the ship

with the family

to see her off.

"Good-bye! Good-bye!" everyone shouted

Harry wagged his tail.

The lady next door started to sing

a good-bye song.

But no one ever heard her.

Just as she sang the first note

the ship blew its foghorn.

It was a deep, low, wonderful sound.

As the ship moved away from the dock,

other boats blew their foghorns too.

Harry thought it was

the most beautiful good-bye song

he had ever heard.

The End

No More Monsters for Me!

by Peggy Parish
pictures by Marc Simont

HarperCollins*Publishers*

"Not even a tadpole,

Minneapolis Simpkin,"

yelled Mom.

"And I mean it!"

"Okay, okay,"

I yelled back.

5

Mom and I always yell a lot.

But this time,

she was really mad.

And so was I.

I stamped out of the house.

I did not care

what Mom said.

I was going to have a pet.

I would take a long walk

and think about this.

So I walked

down the road.

Suddenly I heard

a funny noise.

The noise came

from the bushes.

I stopped and listened.

"Something is crying,
Minneapolis Simpkin,"
I said to myself.
"I will find out

what it is."

I looked in the bushes.

Was I surprised!

"Wow! A baby monster!"

I yelled.

I looked at the monster.

It looked at me.

Then it ran to me.

I put my arms around it.

"Don't cry," I said.

"Minneapolis Simpkin
will help you."

The monster stopped crying.

We stood there
hugging each other.

"A monster for a pet?"

I asked.

Mom never said no

to a monster.

But I never asked her that.

Will she say yes?

I needed time

to think about this.

But there was no time.

It started raining.

The monster did not like it.

It started bawling.

And I do mean bawling!

"Okay, okay," I said.

I grabbed the monster.

I ran home with it.

Mom was in the kitchen.

She did not see me.

But she heard me.

"Are you wet?" she asked.

"Yes," I said.

"Hurry and get dry,"
she said.

"Supper is about ready."

I ran to my room.

"So far, so good,"
I said to myself.

"But what now,
Minneapolis Simpkin?"

I shook my head.

I did not know.

"Minn," yelled Mom,

"supper is ready."

"Coming," I yelled back.

I started to go down.

The monster came, too.

"No," I said.

"You can't come."

I put the monster

in my closet.

It started bawling again.

What was I going to do?

I looked all around.

"My teddy bear!" I said.

I got the teddy bear.

"Here," I said.

The monster grabbed the bear.

It stopped crying.

I ran down to supper.

Mom had made a good supper.

Then I thought of something.

Monsters have to eat, too.

"Mom," I said,

"what do monsters eat?"

"Food, I guess," said Mom.

"But what kind?" I asked.

"Oh," said Mom.

"Is this a new game?"

Mom loves to play games.

So I said, "Yes."

"Let me think," said Mom.

"What *do* monsters eat?"

I was glad to let her think,

because I saw something.

I saw the monster.

"I will be right back,"

I yelled.

"I have to get something."

I had to get something, all right.

I had to get the monster hidden.

I grabbed the monster.

I took it to the basement.

The monster started crying again.

"Quiet!" I said.

"If Mom hears you,

we are in for it."

I grabbed an apple.

"Here," I said.

The monster took the apple.

It stopped crying.

I grabbed another apple.

I ran back to the table.

"Here, Mom," I said.

I gave the apple to her.

"What is this for?"

she asked.

I didn't know what to say.

But I had to say something.

"Because I love you," I said.

Mom laughed.

"Minneapolis Simpkin," she said,

"I love you, too."

Then Mom said, "Pickles!"

"Pickles?" I said.

"Of course," said Mom.

"Monsters love pickles."

"I didn't know that," I said.

Then I asked,

"Do you know where monsters live?"

"Yes," said Mom.

"They live in caves.

Deep dark caves."

"Gee, Mom," I said.

"You know a lot about monsters."

"I love monster stories,"

said Mom.

"I read lots of them."

Did Mom like real monsters, too?

I started to ask her.

But I didn't.

The basement door was opening.

"I will be right back, Mom,"

I yelled.

"Minneapolis Simpkin!"

yelled Mom.

"Can't you sit still?"

"Hic-cup, hic-cup!"

Oh, no!

The monster had hiccups.

"Now you have the hiccups,"

yelled Mom.

"I will get some water,"

I yelled back.

"HIC-CUP! HIC-CUP!"

I opened the basement door.

My eyes almost popped out.

"You grew!" I yelled.

"What did you say?"

asked Mom.

"Nothing," I said.

I pushed the monster

back into the basement.

It was awful.

The monster was huge.

It was lumpy.

"HIC-CUP! HIC-CUP!"

I got some water.

"Drink this," I said.

The monster drank the water.

The hiccups stopped.

"Minn," yelled Mom,

"please bring me

another apple."

"Okay," I yelled back.

But there were

no more apples.

Now I knew

why the monster was lumpy.

I grabbed a potato.

The monster

grabbed it from me.

I grabbed another one

and ran.

I locked the basement door.

"Here, Mom," I said.

"Minn, this is a potato,"

said Mom.

"I asked for an apple."

"Oh, sorry, Mom," I said.

"Minn," said Mom,

"why are you so jumpy?

Is something wrong?"

Something wrong?

Was it ever!

But maybe Mom could help.

So I said, "I am fine.

Tell me some more about monsters.

Where are those caves?"

"Up in the hills," said Mom.

"But don't bother

to look for one."

"Why not?" I asked.

"They are all hidden," she said.

"Only monsters can find them."

"Are you sure?" I asked.

"That is what
my mother told me,"
said Mom.

"I looked and I looked.
I never could find one."

I sure hoped Mom was right.

I had to get that monster home.

It was not a good pet.

Then it happened.

CRASH!

Mom jumped up.

"What was that?"

she asked.

Then she looked at me.

"Minn," she said,

"you were in the basement."

I nodded my head.

"Did you bring home

an animal?"

I nodded my head again.

"Minneapolis Simpkin!"

yelled Mom.

"I said NO PETS!"

"It is not a pet!"

I yelled back.

"Then what is it?"

yelled Mom.

I did not mean to.

I did not want to.

But I started bawling.

"It is a monster!"

I bawled.

I waited for

Mom to yell.

But she didn't.

"Oh, Minn," she said.
"You really need a pet,
don't you?"
"Yes," I bawled.

"But I want a kitten

or a puppy.

I don't want a monster."

"No," said Mom.

"A monster is not a good pet."

I stopped bawling.

"Now," said Mom,

"go and close that window."

"Window! What window?"

I asked.

"The basement window,"

said Mom.

"I must have left it open."

I just looked at her.

I still did not understand.

"Minneapolis Simpkin!"

said Mom.

"The wind is blowing hard.

It blew something over.

That is what made the noise.

Go close the window."

I went.

There was a window open.

The potato basket

was turned over.

The potatoes were all gone.

But the monster

was still there.

It was sleeping.

I looked at it.

How would I ever

get it out of the basement?

It was getting

bigger and bigger.

I went back to Mom.

"I closed the window,"

I said.

"The monster is there.

But it is sleeping."

"Okay, Minn, you win,"

said Mom.

"I was wrong.

I will make a deal.

You get rid of your monster,

and you can have

a real pet.

Deal?"

"Deal!" I cried.

That monster was no pet.

But it was real.

"Good," said Mom.

"I am going to take

a long bath.

You get rid of

your monster."

"Sure, Mom," I said.

I was not sure.

But I was sure

going to try.

I woke up the monster.

"Come on," I said.

"We are going."

The monster came.

It had to crawl
through the doors.
And I had to push
from behind.
But we made it.
I headed for the hills.
The monster followed.

The night was very dark.

I don't like the dark.

But I had to get

that monster home.

We got to the hills.

The monster looked at them.

It made happy noises.

"Is this your home?"

I asked.

The monster turned to me.

Suddenly

we were hugging each other.

Then the monster

ran up the hill.

I felt good.

The monster

had found its home.

"No more monsters for me,"

I said.

I ran all the way home.

Mom was yelling for me.

I went into the house.

"Minneapolis Simpkin!"

yelled Mom.

"Where have you been?"

"Getting rid of the monster,"

I yelled back.

"That is what
you told me to do."
I started to bawl again.
Mom looked at me
in a funny way.
She hugged me.

Then I knew.

I knew Mom didn't believe

that monster was real.

But Mom kept our deal.

We went to the pet shop.

Mom really surprised me.

She bought two kittens.

"Two!" I said.

"Sure," said Mom.

"One for you,

and one for me."

"Mom," I said,

"you are okay."

"And so are you, Minn,"
said Mom.
We each took a kitten.
And we went home.

I Can Read!

BEGINNING
1
READING

MORRIS
THE MOOSE

by B. Wiseman

HarperCollins*Publishers*

One day

Morris the Moose

saw a cow.

"You are

a funny-looking moose,"

he said.

"I am a COW.

I am not a MOOSE!"

said the cow.

"You have four legs

and a tail

and things on your head," said Morris.

"You are a moose."

"But I say MOO!"

said the cow.

8

"I can say MOO too!"

said Morris.

The cow said,

"I give MILK to people."

"So you are a moose
who gives milk to people!"
said Morris.

"But my mother

is a COW!"

said the cow.

"You are a MOOSE,"
said Morris.
"So your mother
must be a moose too!"

13

"What can I tell you?"
the cow said.
"You can tell me
you are a moose,"
said Morris.

"No!" cried the cow.

"I am NOT a moose!

Ask him.

He will tell you

what I am."

"What is she?"

Morris asked the deer.

The deer said,

"She has four legs

and a tail

and things on her head.

She is a deer, like me."

"She is a MOOSE, like ME!"
Morris yelled.

"You?

You are not a moose.

You are a deer too!"

The deer laughed.

"I am a MOOSE!"

cried Morris.

"You are a DEER!"

shouted the deer.

"What can I tell you?"
asked Morris.
"You can tell me
you are a deer,"
said the deer.

"Let's ask
somebody else,"
said the cow.

"Okay, Moose," said Morris the Moose.

"Okay, Deer," said the deer.

They walked until
they found a horse.

"Hello, you horses!"

said the horse.

"What are those funny things

on your heads?"

"Oh, dear." The cow sighed.

"Let's ask somebody else.

But first let's get a drink."

Morris, the cow, and the deer
drank from a cool, blue stream.

Morris looked at himself

in the water and smiled.

"You two do not look

at all like me," he said.

"You cannot be moose."

"You mean,

you are not DEER,"

said the deer.

"You don't look

at all like me."

"See?" said the cow.

"I am not a moose

or a deer.

I am a COW!

You made a MISTAKE."

"I did not," said Morris.

"I made a MOOSEtake!"